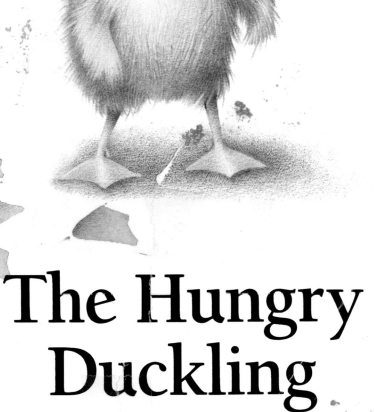

# The Hungry Duckling

Claude Clément
Adapted by Deborah Kovacs
Illustrations by Marcelle Geneste

Reader's Digest Kids
Pleasantville, N.Y.–Montreal

"What a warm spring we're having!" said Mother Duck, fanning herself.

"Why don't you go for a swim to cool off?" asked Mother Hen. "I'll sit on your egg for you. I'm just waiting for my own to hatch."

"Oh thank you!" cried Mother Duck. "I'll be back soon." And so Mother Duck waddled to the pond for a short swim.

That's how a little duckling came to be born into a family of chicks.

When Mother Hen saw that all the eggs had hatched, she taught the duckling and the chicks how to walk up and down the henhouse ramp to stretch their tiny legs.

"What a funny waddle he has!" said one little chick, pointing to the duckling. "He must have been in his egg too long!"

"No," said Mother Hen gently. "He is a little duckling, not a hen chick like the rest of you. If you visit the duck pond, you will see that all ducks waddle like that."

When it was time to eat, Mother Hen showed her little ones some tasty grain that was spread on the ground. The chicks pecked at it until they were full. But the little duckling's bill was too big and round to pick up the tiny bits of grain.

"I'm so hungry," he said to one of the chicks. "Do you know what ducks eat?"

"No, I don't," answered the chick.

"I guess I'll have to find out for myself," said the hungry duckling. He waddled down the path, searching for a good meal.

The first creature the little duckling met
was a round gray snail. "I'm so hungry,"
said the little duckling. "Do you know
what ducks eat?"

"No, I don't," said the snail. "But I eat
crunchy leaves. Try some."

The hungry duckling tried to bite into
the leaves with his flat bill, but he couldn't
chew them. "I guess ducks don't eat
leaves," he sighed as he waddled farther
down the path.

Soon, he met a frog. "I'm so hungry," said the duckling to the frog. "Do you know what ducks eat?"

"No, I don't," said the frog. "But I eat flies. Try one." With that, the frog shot out his long, sticky tongue and caught a fly, swallowing it in one gulp. But the little duckling's tongue was too short to catch a fly.

"I guess ducks don't eat flies," he said, watching the frog bound across the wildflowers.

Before long, the hungry duckling arrived at the pond. There was Mother Duck, just finishing her swim. "My little duckling!" quacked Mother Duck in surprise. "You hatched early! It's such a hot day. Hop in the pond with me!"

"I don't want to go swimming. I'm too hungry," said the little duckling. And before his mother could help him, he started to waddle away, looking for something to eat.

At that moment, a little kingfisher, who had been sitting in a nearby tree, dove into the pond. "You won't go in the pond?" he teased. "You're a chicken!"

"No, I'm not! I'm a duck!" said the little duckling proudly, and he dove in after him.

The duckling watched as the kingfisher gobbled up the little minnows, worms, and tadpoles at the bottom of the pond. The little duckling's tummy began to growl and he felt very, very hungry.

"Try some!" called the kingfisher.

So the little duckling tried some. "This is delicious!" he told the kingfisher. "This must be what ducks eat!"

At the end of the day, the little duckling waddled back to the barnyard with his mother, full of food and ready for bed. "I'm glad you're not a hungry duckling anymore," said Mother Duck.

"I'm a sleepy duckling now," yawned the duckling. "Do you know where ducks sleep?"

"Yes, I do, my little one," Mother Duck replied, tucking him under her warm wing. "Good night."

Duck eggs must be kept very warm, so a mother duck can leave them only for short periods of time to eat or swim.

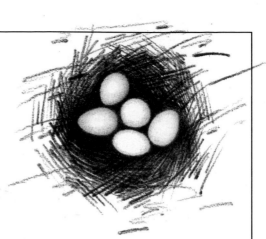

Ducks love water. That's why they often make their homes alongside ponds and beaches. Thanks to their webbed feet, they are very good swimmers.

Ducks have big flat beaks. At the edge of their beaks are ridges that filter the water they drink.